COOKIE'S WEEK

by Cindy Ward

illustrated by Tomie dePaola

Penguin Young Readers Group

For Paul, who started it all;
for Dr. Eagling and staff, who kept it going;
and, always, for Rodney,
who never turns away a stray. —C W

For all the staff at Russell Animal Hospital,
who like Satie in spite of everything. —T D E P

Text copyright © 1988 by Cindy Ward
Illustrations copyright © 1988 by Tomie dePaola. All rights reserved.
This book, or parts thereof, may not be reproduced
in any form without permission in writing from the publisher.
A PaperStar Book, published in 1997 by Penguin Putnam
Books for Young Readers, 345 Hudson Street, New York, NY 10014.
PaperStar Books is a registered trademark of The Putnam Berkley Group, Inc.
The PaperStar logo is a registered trademark of The Putnam Berkley Group, Inc.
Originally published in 1988 by G. P. Putnam's Sons. Published
simultaneously in Canada. Manufactured in China
Library of Congress Cataloging-in-Publication Data
Ward, Cindy. Cookie's week. Summary: Cookie the cat gets into a different
kind of mischief every day or the week. [i. Cats—Fiction. 2.Days—Fiction.]
I. dePaola, Tomie, ill. II. Title. PZ7.W187Co 1988 [E]87-25497
ISBN 978-0-698-11435-7

On Monday...

Cookie fell in the toilet.

There was water everywhere!

On Tuesday...

Cookie knocked a plant
off the windowsill.

There was dirt everywhere!

On Wednesday…

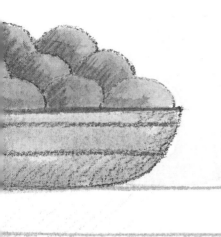

Cookie upset the trash can.

There was garbage everywhere!

On Thursday...

Cookie got stuck in a kitchen drawer.

There were pots and pans
and dishes everywhere!

On Friday...

Cookie ran into the closet
before the door closed.

There were clothes everywhere!

On Saturday...

Cookie climbed the curtains.

And Cookie *went* everywhere!

Tomorrow is Sunday…

Maybe Cookie will rest!